THE LEGENDS OF KING ARTHUR
MERLIN, MAGIC AND DRAGONS

Dados Internacionais de Catalogação na Publicação (CIP) de acordo com ISBD

M469l   Mayhew, Tracey
         Lancelot / adaptado por Tracey Mayhew. – Jandira : W. Books, 2025.
         96 p. ; 12,8cm x 19,8cm. – (The legends of king Arthur)

         ISBN: 978-65-5294-168-8

             1. Literatura infantojuvenil. 2. Literatura Infantil. 3. Clássicos. 4. Literatura
inglesa. 5. Lendas. 6. Folclore. 7. Mágica. 8. Cultura Popular. I. Título. II. Série.

2025-615   CDD 028.5
                                                       CDU 82-93

Elaborado por Vagner Rodolfo da Silva - CRB-8/9410
Índice para catálogo sistemático:
1. Literatura infantojuvenil 028.5
2. Literatura infantojuvenil 82-93

The Legends of King Arthur: Merlin, Magic, and Dragons
Text © Sweet Cherry Publishing Limited, 2020
Inside illustrations © Sweet Cherry Publishing Limited, 2020
Cover illustrations © Sweet Cherry Publishing Limited, 2020

Text by Tracey Mayhew
Illustrations by Mike Phillips

© 2025 edition:
Ciranda Cultural Editora e Distribuidora Ltda.

1st edition in 2025
www.cirandacultural.com.br
No part of this publication may be reproduced, stored in a retrieval
system, or transmitted in any form or by any means, electronic,
mechanical, photocopying, recording, or otherwise, without written
permission of the publisher.
This book is a work of fiction. Names, characters, places, and incidents
are either the product of the author's imagination or are used fictitiously,
and any resemblance to actual persons, living or dead, business
establishments, events, or locales is entirely coincidental.

The Legends of King Arthur

Lancelot

Retold by
Tracey Mayhew

Illustrated by
Mike Phillips

W. Books

Chapter One

Lancelot reined his horse to a stop as he reached the edge of the woods. Camelot appeared gracefully in the distance. Beside Lancelot, his best friend Gawain's horse stamped at the cold ground impatiently.

'What's the matter?' Gawain asked.

'Nothing.'

'Then why have you stopped?' Gawain pointed to a third horse. The stag they had hunted lay draped across its back. 'We must get this back for the feast.'

'Go on ahead,' Lancelot said. 'I will follow.'

Frowning, Gawain asked,
'Is something wrong?
You've been quiet lately.'

'I'm fine.'

'If you're sure …' Gawain didn't
believe him, but knew that Lancelot
would say no more. He continued on
to Camelot, leading the other horse
behind him.

Lancelot sighed. Gawain was
right. He hadn't been himself lately
and there was only one reason for
it: Guinevere. Lancelot knew his
feelings were wrong. They were
a betrayal of his king, a man
who had quickly become
his friend. But from the

moment he had arrived in Camelot, Lancelot had loved its queen. Over the past four years, his love for her had only grown stronger. With no word from Tristan this past year, he hadn't even had their jousting competitions to distract him.

Looking at Camelot now, Lancelot did not really want to return. It was a place he had come to call home, yet being there caused him increasing pain. Reminding himself that the pain of leaving would be even greater, Lancelot gently nudged his horse. As they continued their slow approach, he thought about what had first brought him to Arthur's court.

As a child Lancelot had sat at his father's feet, listening to his stories of war and the many battles he had fought. Lancelot had decided then that when he was old enough, he would fight alongside his father. But fate had stepped in.

Lancelot had been only six summers old when he saw his father killed by his enemy, King Claudas. One of his earliest memories was of his mother hiding him in a secret chamber. He had watched through a spyhole as she

pleaded for her life. Then she, too, had been killed. Terrified, Lancelot had run from his father's castle that night. He had only stopped when a mysterious woman stepped into his path.

The Lady of the Lake had saved Lancelot, offering him safety in the magical land of Avalon. It was there he had learnt the skills needed to become the greatest knight the world had ever known.

When Lancelot had turned eighteen, the Lady of the Lake had taken him to Camelot. There he was given a place at King Arthur's Round Table.

Later, Lancelot had been introduced to Queen Guinevere, and had fallen deeply in love with her. But it was no good – Guinevere only had eyes for her husband. That was how it should be, but knowing that didn't make it any less painful for him.

Now Lancelot looked for any excuse to get away from Camelot, if only for a few hours. He knew he should leave for good. He needed to put as much distance between himself and the woman he loved so that he may, in time, forget her. But he couldn't.

Chapter Two

The following day, Lancelot rode out with his friend Sir Lionel. Sir Lionel was looking for adventure as much as Lancelot was looking for distraction. All day they rode through the borderlands of Wales, only stopping when they were too tired to ride farther.

'We can make camp there,' said Sir Lionel, pointing towards a tree not far away.

Lancelot agreed, fighting back a yawn. 'We've got food, too,' he declared, once he had reached the tree and plucked an

apple from the lowest branch. He took a bite and enjoyed its sharp tang.

After tying up their horses, Lionel took first watch. It wasn't long before Lancelot fell asleep. As the night went on, Lionel began to fight the need to sleep as well. He tried not to, but eventually his head began to droop, and his eyes drifted shut …

Lionel was ripped from sleep by a strange sound – a cry of pain? – in the distance. He moved to wake Lancelot but changed his mind. If Lancelot came with him, Lancelot would deal with the source of the sound. Then Lionel's own chance of adventure would be gone. No, Lionel decided, he would deal with this himself.

Lionel untied his horse and led him to the edge of the clearing before mounting. As he rode away, he strained his ears to hear more. Eventually, he did: it was the sound of horses' hooves pounding the ground.

And it was getting closer.

Suddenly, three horses burst out of the trees and onto the path ahead of him. Each horse carried two passengers: a rider, and a prisoner draped facedown across its withers. As one of the men begged for his release, a fourth rider appeared on the path, dressed head-to-toe in black armour. He laughed cruelly at the prisoners.

'You have learnt this lesson the hard way: *no one is stronger than Turquyn.* I am the greatest knight of the Borderlands!'

Spurring his horse into action, Lionel overtook the four horses and blocked their path.

'Stop!' Lionel cried.

The black-armoured knight – Turquyn – reined his horse to a stop. 'And who are you to make such a command?' he asked.

'I am Sir Lionel of the Round Table!' Lionel declared. 'I demand you release these men!'

Turquyn laughed. 'Oh, you do, do you? Well, Sir Lionel, I *will* release them.' He drew his sword. 'But only if you defeat me.'

Drawing his own sword, Lionel brought it down hard and fast towards Turquyn. The next thing he knew, he was on the ground, and Turquyn was kicking his sword out of reach.

Tearing Lionel's helmet from his head, Turquyn stood over him, blade levelled at his throat. 'Do you surrender, Knight of the Round Table?'

Lionel glared. He had not expected to fall so quickly, nor so easily. He had not expected to fall at all! With no other option, Lionel nodded his surrender.

Turquyn smiled, stepping back to drag Lionel to his feet. Seizing the chance, Lionel made a grab for

Turquyn's sword. But again, somehow, he was too slow. Turquyn's fist was almost a blur as he pulled it back and landed a heavy blow to the side of Lionel's head.

Lionel fell back to the ground, even more dazed than before. He tried to push himself to his feet but gave up as the world began to spin. Eventually, everything went black.

Lionel opened his eyes and groaned. His head felt like it had been split in two. When he tried to move, he found that his hands and feet were tied.

'It's no use,' said a familiar voice nearby.

Lionel struggled into a sitting position. 'Gareth? You've been gone from Camelot so long we thought you must have found a wife!'

Gareth chuckled bitterly. 'Alas, no. I've been a prisoner here for … I've lost count of the days! And we're not alone. There are others in other cells: ordinary men as well as knights.'

'Who?'

'I heard Kay and Geraint shouting, although they've given up now they know there's no one listening.'

Hearing the hopelessness in his friend's voice, Lionel wanted to lift his spirits. 'There is hope yet,' he insisted. 'I was with Lancelot before being captured. He will find us, I'm sure of it.'

'Lancelot, you say?' Gareth asked eagerly. 'If anyone can save us, it's him. Where is he?'

Lionel hesitated for a moment. 'I left him sleeping under an apple tree.'

His words were greeted with silence. Gareth slumped unhappily. 'Then there is no hope.'

Lionel could only hope he was wrong.

Chapter Three

The night passed and Lancelot slept on, unaware of anything outside his dreams of Guinevere. Not even the passing of three ladies and their knights could wake him, although two of the three ladies stopped to admire his face.

'Who is he do you think?' Lady Ara whispered to her sister.

'He looks like a knight,' Lady Sabrina replied, her gaze fixed upon the stranger. 'He is rather handsome.'

'He will make a fine husband, I am sure of it,' Ara murmured, already imagining the handsome stranger by her side.

Sabrina glared at her. 'Let's not forget, sister, that I saw him first.'

Before Ara could reply, the third lady guided her horse over to the bickering sisters. Looking upon the knight, she recognised him immediately. Her son, Mordred, had been a squire at Camelot for almost a year. Thanks to his many secret reports, Morgan le Fay knew that it was Lancelot du Lac who lay at their feet.

'Do not argue over him, my friends,' she said. 'Instead, let us take him to my castle where he may choose between you.'

Morgan smiled. She would use this unexpected change of events to ensure that Lancelot would never return to Camelot. Arthur would lose his greatest knight.

Giggling excitedly, the two sisters didn't notice as Morgan knelt down beside the sleeping knight. She waved a hand over him and whispered an enchantment that would keep him asleep for many hours to come.

♣

Opening his eyes, Lancelot blinked into the gloom, shivering against the dampness that was settling into his bones. He frowned when he realised he was no longer wearing his armour and his sword was gone. As he looked

around, squinting into the shadows, he realised he was in a dungeon. He had been taken prisoner! How had this happened? He had only slept for a moment. And where was Lionel? His friend could be in another cell, or worse, dead.

Leaping to his feet, Lancelot flew to the heavy wooden door and pounded on it until the wooden hatch was yanked open.

'You're awake then?' grunted the guard.

'Where am I?' Lancelot demanded.

'My lady is on her way.'

The hatch slammed shut once more. Soon, however, the guard returned. He stepped into Lancelot's cell with three ladies.

Lancelot stood, his eyes taking in each lady in turn. Two of the three had pretty faces and warm smiles, but the third looked at him with dark eyes that seemed to hate him. She, unlike the other ladies, was dressed in black, and fiery red hair framed her face.

'We know that you are Lancelot du Lac, the greatest knight in Britain,' she began, as the ladies behind her giggled. 'But here you are defenseless and at my mercy.'

'And who are you, my lady?' Lancelot asked. Something about this woman unsettled him.

The lady shook her head. 'That does not matter. All you need to know is that these ladies love you, and both would have you as their husband.

You must choose between them or die a slow and painful death.'

Lancelot swallowed nervously. An image of Guinevere appeared in his mind and he shook his head. 'I am sorry, but I hold only one woman in my heart. I am sworn to her and her alone.' He faced the two women, whose eyes now shone with tears. 'I cannot marry either of you.'

At his words, they ran crying from the cell. The third woman remained, smiling coldly. 'Well, Sir Lancelot, you have made your choice. Now all that's left is for me to make mine. How shall I kill you?' she mused, making her own slow way to the door.

There she paused. She looked back. 'I shall enjoy causing you pain.'

And with that, she left, the guard slamming the door behind her.

In the darkness of his cell, Lancelot lost track of time. How many days had passed? Or was it weeks? Was he being fed once a day? Twice?

It was always the same maidservant who brought his food, so this time when a key rattled in the door, he knew who to expect. Sure enough, the young lady swept in, but with no food and more panic than usual.

'My lord, there is no time to waste!' she whispered, beckoning him towards her.

Crossing the cell, Lancelot followed her outside. He kept to the

shadows of the corridor. 'Where's the guard?' he asked.

'Don't worry about him,' the maidservant said, as she led him farther into the depths of the castle. There the corridors became more like tunnels, with low ceilings and close walls. Lancelot had to duck his head

and turn his shoulders to squeeze through, but eventually they spilled into daylight. It stung Lancelot's eyes after so long in the dark.

Outside, a young stable hand was waiting with a horse and Lancelot's sword and armour. Once he was dressed and armed, Lancelot mounted

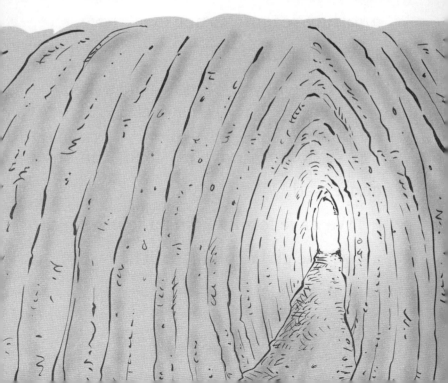

his horse. 'Why would you do this?' he asked the maidservant. 'Why risk your life for me?'

The maidservant looked up at him. 'The lady of this castle is a cruel, wicked woman,' she explained. 'We have no loyalty to her.'

Lancelot nodded, but he saw another reason in her eyes: love. Love for him.

'What will you do now?' he asked both of them.

'We do not know, my lord,' the boy confessed.

'We have family living a few villages away,' the girl explained. 'They will take us in.'

Bowing his head, Lancelot said, 'I owe my life to you, my lady. Thank you.'

After a quick nod of thanks to the boy, Lancelot spurred his horse, leaving the castle and its evil mistress behind.

Chapter Four

That night Lancelot rode as far as he could. At dawn, he set off again. He was eager to get as far away from the castle as possible before his escape was discovered.

Approaching a clearing, Lancelot paused at the sound of voices. He dismounted and tied his horse to the nearest tree. Then he crept towards the edge of the clearing. Immediately, he recognized the golden, two-headed eagle painted on the shield of the knight farthest from him: Sir Gaheris!

Opposite him was an enormous, black-armoured knight. Both men's swords were drawn. Lancelot remained hidden as he watched the duel unfold.

Gaheris blocked the black knight's first attack and returned it quickly and ferociously. The black knight did not

even carry a shield, but deflected each blow easily as Gaheris began to tire.

Unable to stand by and watch any longer, Lancelot drew his own sword. He was about to step out from his hiding place, when Gaheris was dealt a heavy blow that sent him crashing to the ground.

'Do you surrender?' the black knight demanded, kicking Gaheris' sword out of reach.

Lancelot couldn't hear his friend's reply but his enemy seemed satisfied. He removed his black helmet and knelt to bind his prisoner's hands together. He began dragging Gaheris towards his horse when he caught sight of Lancelot stepping out from the trees.

'Release him,' Lancelot demanded.

At the familiar voice, Gaheris looked up. He smiled in relief. The black-armoured knight laughed. 'And who are you to demand that of me?'

'I am Lancelot du Lac, Knight of the Round Table.'

The black knight dropped Gaheris. He was broader and taller than Lancelot and was clearly a fierce warrior, but Lancelot was not afraid. He had fought bigger men than himself on many occasions and lived to tell the tale.

Picking up speed, Lancelot attacked the black knight. He landed a well-aimed strike upon the knight's left arm before twisting away from his opponent's counter-attack and striking his sword arm. For a moment, the black knight's grip on his sword faltered but he quickly recovered.

'At last, I have a worthy opponent!' he declared. 'It will be an honour to defeat a man like you!'

At his words, Lancelot launched another ferocious attack. The black knight was driven back, too busy defending himself to retaliate. Finally, Lancelot swung his sword in a final strike. The blade arced through the

air and easily sliced through the black knight's neck. The knight fell to the ground, his blood soaking into the grass at Lancelot's feet.

Stepping back, Lancelot wiped his blade before making his way over to Gaheris.

'Am I glad to see you!' Gaheris laughed as Lancelot untied him. 'I thought all hope was lost!'

Lancelot smiled. 'Hope is never lost, my friend. What are doing out here?'

'King Arthur sent some of us to look for the knights that have gone missing.'

'Missing?'

Gaheris nodded, pushing himself to his feet. 'You, Lionel, Kay and Geraint.'

'Who else is with you?' Lancelot asked.

Gaheris shook his head. 'No one. We split up. That's when I came across him.' He pointed his blade towards the dead knight. 'He said he had already defeated other Knights of the Round Table.'

After retrieving their horses, the two knights headed south until they came to a huge tree on the path ahead of them. From each branch hung a shield, many of which the knights recognised.

'That's Sir Kay's shield,' Lancelot murmured.

'And Sir Lionel's. The black knight has displayed them like trophies!' Gaheris sounded disgusted.

'Which must mean that he lived around here somewhere.'

Sure enough, the two knights soon discovered

a round tower in the middle of a clearing. It appeared to be unguarded and quiet.

'Do you think this is it?' Gaheris asked.

Lancelot shrugged. 'We will not know unless we look.'

Dismounting, the two knights approached the tower with their weapons drawn. They entered it cautiously, and were surprised to find it was deserted. A set of stairs led them down into the dungeons. At the bottom they heard Kay's gruff voice coming from behind the nearest door.

'Kay?' Lancelot cried.

'Lancelot? Get us of out of here!'

'Lancelot, here!' Gaheris called, throwing a bunch of keys he had found.

Lancelot caught them easily and unlocked Kay's door. Kay and Geraint burst into the corridor. It wasn't long before every other man was free too.

'Take them all back to Camelot,'
Lancelot instructed the knights.

'What about you?' Lionel asked.
'Aren't you coming with us?'

Lancelot shook his head as an image
of Guinevere appeared in his mind. He
was not ready to return. 'No, not yet.'

Lionel nodded. 'I hope
you find whatever it is
you're looking for.'

Lancelot smiled before
leading his horse back
into the forest, ready for
his next adventure.

Chapter Five

The forest Lancelot rode through seemed to wither as he went. Ghostly trees with branches like bones replaced what had been bright and green before. The light faded, even though it was still the middle of the day. The air grew cold and damp, making Lancelot shiver beneath his tunic and armour. Everywhere he looked was deserted, dark and dismal. A dying wasteland.

Lancelot soon came across a castle that looked every bit as deserted and

broken as its surroundings. It towered over everything, beautiful despite the crumbling walls encircling it.

Lancelot's horse edged forward, clearly unsure. Crossing the moss-covered bridge that led to the gatehouse, Lancelot was met by two guards with spears planted on the ground. They, too, looked as though they had seen better days.

After announcing who he was, the two men led Lancelot through the castle to their master's Great Hall. There men

and women sat talking at long tables that ran the length of the room. At the head of the hall, on a low platform, sat a weary-looking old man with long, thinning white hair. His dirty clothes hung off him. His heavily bandaged leg had been raised on a stool, and a branch fashioned into a crutch was propped up against the side of his throne. His eyes alone shone brightly,

seeming younger than the rest of him. He smiled as Lancelot entered.

'And who do we have here?' he rasped weakly.

'My name is Lancelot du Lac, my lord.' Lancelot bowed.

'Then I welcome you, Sir Lancelot, to the castle of the Maimed King.' Seeing Lancelot's confusion, he added, 'I am

King Pelles, King of the Wasteland and of this haunted place, Corbenic.' He held his arms wide, as if presenting the castle. 'Please, take a seat. I would stand to greet you but …'

Lancelot smiled and took the seat that Pelles offered. His heart sank as he realised no food or drink had been laid out on the table. After his long journey and his fight with the black

knight, his stomach was growling. But he said nothing.

'You are just in time, Lancelot,' Pelles told him.

'In time for what?'

Just then a set of doors at one end of the Great Hall opened. Everyone inside grew quiet. In walked three women wearing white, hooded robes that hid their faces. Lancelot watched as they slowly made their way down the centre of the hall.

The first woman carried a spear, the tip of which dripped blood. With each step another red droplet would fall, but as she drew closer to Lancelot, he saw that none had actually hit the flagstone floor.

Lancelot's gaze shifted to the second woman, who carried a silver tray. It was the third woman, however, who finally held his and everyone else's attention. She walked behind the others, carrying what seemed to be a cup. It was covered by a white cloth. A golden light shone through the cloth, bathing the woman in a holy light. Lancelot found himself joining the rest of Pelles's guests in prayer as the three women continued their journey through the Great Hall to the doors at the other end.

Hearing the thud of the solid oak as it closed behind them, Lancelot finished his prayer and looked up.

'Do you know what you have just witnessed?' Pelles asked him. Lancelot could only shake his head. 'My friend, that was the Grail procession. The spear you saw was the spear that pierced Our Lord Jesus Christ's side as he hung upon the cross. The tray was the one he ate from at the Last Supper. The cup was the Holy Grail, which my ancestor caught Christ's sacred blood in.'

Lancelot's gaze was fixed on the door the three women had left through. The sun still shone outside the windows and yet the hall seemed darker without the heavenly glow of the Holy Grail. He wondered if he would ever see it again.

Pelles seemed to read his thought. 'One day,' he said, 'the Grail will appear in Camelot. When it does, every knight will ride out to prove himself worthy of it.'

Lancelot nodded. He must return to Camelot before that day came. But not yet …

Chapter Six

Lancelot remained at Corbenic long enough for King Pelles's daughter, Elaine, to fall deeply in love with him. But even if Lancelot had known of her

feelings, he could not have returned them. His heart belonged to Guinevere.

Pelles reassured his daughter, 'One day, my dear, he will return your love. Have patience and faith.'

Deep down, however, Elaine knew that Lancelot would never return her feelings whilst he loved another. She suffered quietly, until one day an old woman approached her in the Wasteland outside of Corbenic.

'Poor dear,' the old woman said. 'I see a man has captured your heart.'

Elaine sniffed, wiping away a tear. 'How did you know?'

'I know many things,' the old woman replied. 'Would you tell me about him? I may be able to help.'

Elaine's heart soared. She longed to talk about Lancelot, to tell someone how much she loved him. And how wonderful would it be if this old woman could help her?

What Elaine did not know was that this old woman was actually Morgan le Fay in disguise. Morgan had been searching for the knight she had lost; the knight she hoped would be the key to King Arthur's downfall. Her magic had led her here, to King Pelles's castle, and Elaine's tale of unrequited love.

When Elaine had

finished, Morgan le Fay studied her. She could sense the strength of Elaine's feelings and knew how desperate she was to win Lancelot's heart. Morgan smiled to herself. She may have lost Lancelot once but she would not lose him again.

'I can help you, my dear,' she murmured.

Elaine's eyes lit up. 'You can?'

Morgan nodded. She drew a small vial of clear liquid from her robe. 'Drink this,' she instructed, handing Elaine the bottle, 'and you will become whomever Lancelot desires most.'

Elaine stared at the bottle. Swallowing nervously, she pulled the cork free and drank the liquid in one go. She frowned at the taste. 'How long before–?'

Her words were cut short as she doubled over in pain. The bottle fell from her hand and smashed on the ground. Falling to her knees, Elaine groaned. Tears of pain streamed down her cheeks as the magic took effect. Elaine's face began to change, the bones cracking and shifting, her blonde hair becoming darker, longer …

All at once, it was over. Slowly, Elaine opened her eyes – blue now instead of brown – and blinked as she rose to her

feet. Except it was no longer Elaine of Corbenic that stood before Morgan. It was Queen Guinevere.

'Has it worked?' Elaine asked in the queen's voice.

Morgan said nothing. She took a looking glass from her robes and held it up. Elaine gasped at her reflection.

She touched her cheek, marvelling at how different she looked. So *this* was the woman Lancelot loved. She was very beautiful.

'Now what?' she asked Morgan.

'Now we put the rest of our plan into action,' Morgan replied.

'Sir Lancelot, I have a message for you.'

Lancelot turned to see a servant approach with a scroll in his hand. 'Thank you,' he said, taking the parchment.

'I was also told to give you this,' the servant added, holding out a ring.

Lancelot's heart stopped as he recognised Guinevere's ring. As the servant left, Lancelot broke the seal and quickly read the words within. Guinevere was waiting for him at Case Castle!

After bidding King Pelles a hasty farewell, Lancelot left Corbenic behind. By sundown, he had arrived at Case Castle and was soon standing before Guinevere. As ever, she took his breath away. Only now she was looking

at him with an expression he had longed to see, but never had before.

'You came!' she gasped, her eyes full of love. 'How I've missed you, Lancelot!'

After so long apart, Lancelot couldn't help himself. He took Guinevere in his arms and kissed her, all thoughts of honour, duty and loyalty to his king forgotten.

Chapter Seven

The following morning, Lancelot awoke to find himself staring not into the eyes of Guinevere, but those of Elaine of Corbenic. Startled, he scrambled away from her.

'What have you done with Guinevere?' he demanded.

Elaine's hands rose to her face and hair, finding both back to normal. She bit her lip. 'I have done nothing, my lord.'

Lancelot pushed himself away from the bed. 'Guinevere was here last night and now she is gone!'

'*I* was here last night,' Elaine insisted, reaching out to him.

Lancelot shook his head. 'I don't understand.'

Knowing she had no other choice, Elaine took a breath and

told him everything. Lancelot listened with growing horror and crushing disappointment.

'But everything I did, I did out of love for you!' Elaine concluded, tears falling down her cheeks.

The world around Lancelot had begun to spin and the walls were closing in. His breath now came in

strangled gasps. He hated himself for what they had done; for betraying his own heart and his love for Guinevere.

He ran from the room, ignoring Elaine's pleas to stay. Then he ran from the castle, her heartbreak ringing in his ears.

As the days and weeks had turned into months, the people of Camelot had missed Lancelot greatly. King Arthur was so worried that he ordered many knights to ride out in search of him.

It was Sir Bors, who, after many weeks, eventually came across the Wasteland. There he spent days searching until he heard a senseless muttering. Following the voice, he found a ragged man sitting under a tree. He recognised him immediately as Sir Lancelot.

Dismounting his horse, Bors slowly approached. 'Cousin?' he murmured gently. 'It is I, Sir Bors.'

Hearing his cousin's name, Lancelot jerked his head round.

Bors hesitated for a moment, unsure what to do. Lancelot was a shadow of his former self: his hair was tangled, his face dirty, and he had lost so much weight that his shirt hung from him.

'Bors?' Lancelot croaked. When Bors nodded, Lancelot seemed to crumble. His shadowed, bloodshot eyes welled with tears.

Saying nothing, Bors went to him and helped him onto his horse. They slowly made their way through the Wasteland.

When they reached a castle, a woman came rushing out to meet them.

'Lancelot!' she cried. 'What has happened to him?'

'I do not know, my lady,' Bors said. 'I think he has lost his mind.'

Elaine looked fearful. 'Take him to Naciens in the nearby chapel!' she cried. 'There is no time to lose. My manservant will show you the way.'

Bors let himself be led to a small chapel not two miles away. There, an old man wearing brown robes greeted them. He took one look at Lancelot

and immediately ordered Bors to carry him to the altar.

After laying Lancelot down upon the stone, Bors stepped back, letting the man pray over his cousin. Suddenly, the tiny church was filled with a warm light as a golden cup appeared above the altar, and above Lancelot.

Removing his helmet, Bors fell to his knees and bowed his head. Just as quickly as it had appeared, the golden light faded, leaving the church in shadow once more.

Bors looked up. His eyes widened at the sight of Lancelot sitting upright on the altar. He was still bedraggled and scruffy, but he looked much more like his old self.

'Where am I?' Lancelot asked, gazing around as if he had just woken from a long sleep. His memories were slowly coming back to him: arriving at Corbenic, meeting King Pelles, seeing the Grail procession, Elaine's trick …

'I came to find you,' Bors explained. 'Camelot has missed you.'

At the mention of Camelot, Lancelot's thoughts moved to Guinevere. If time and distance made no difference to his heart, he might as well be near her.

Turning to the robed man beside him, he bowed. 'Thank you for all you have done for me.' To Bors he said, 'Come, cousin. I have been away from

home too long. It is time I go back.' *Back to the woman I love*, he added silently.

With that the two knights began their long journey, both eager to leave the Wasteland behind them.

Continue the quest with the next book in the series!

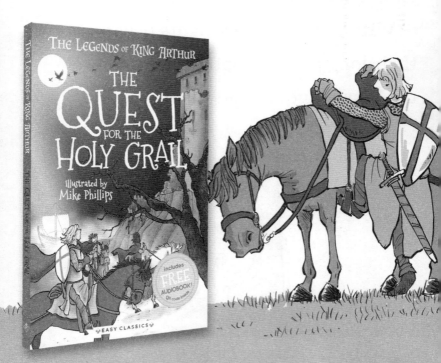

"This series opens the door to a treasure house of wonderful stories which have previously been available chiefly to older readers. We can only welcome it as a fabulous resource for all who love magical tales, and those who will come to love them."

John Matthews
Author of the Red Dragon Rising series and Arthur of Albion